As Big As a Mountain

Annabelle Hartmann

In a country not too far
away from here there
lived a little prince named
Carl. And when I say little,
I mean really, really little.
In fact, he was not much
taller than three large
pieces of cheese piled
on top of each other.

But little Prince Carl
wanted to be **tall**.
His father the king was
tall, his mother the
queen was **tall**. And
everything in the kingdom
was much **bigger**
than him, too. Little Carl
didn`t like being little,
he wanted to be **tall**,
as **tall** as everybody
else. And to make himself
feel a little bit **bigger**,
he wished he could play
with **tall** friends and
huge toys all the time.

For Christoph, Luisa,
Viona and Viktoria

First published in Great Britain in 2003 by
Pavilion Children's Books
A member of Chrysalis Books plc
64 Brewery Road
London N7 9NT
www.pavilionbooks.co.uk

A CIP catalogue record for this book is available from the British Library

ISBN 1 84365 001 0
Set in Sand

Manufactured in China by Imago

2 4 6 8 10 9 7 5 3 1

This book can be ordered direct from the publisher. Please contact
the marketing department. But try your bookshop first.

One day, which happened
to be the very day before
Carl's third birthday, his
father the king asked him:

"Little Carl, what do you
want for your birthday?"

Carl had been waiting
all day for this question.
He took a deep breath
and said excitedly...

"I want a sailing boat as **big** as a **lake!**"

But the king shook his head and said:

"No Carl, you can't have that. If the boat was that **big**, there wouldn't be any water left to sail it in."

"Hmmm." Carl hesitated for a moment.

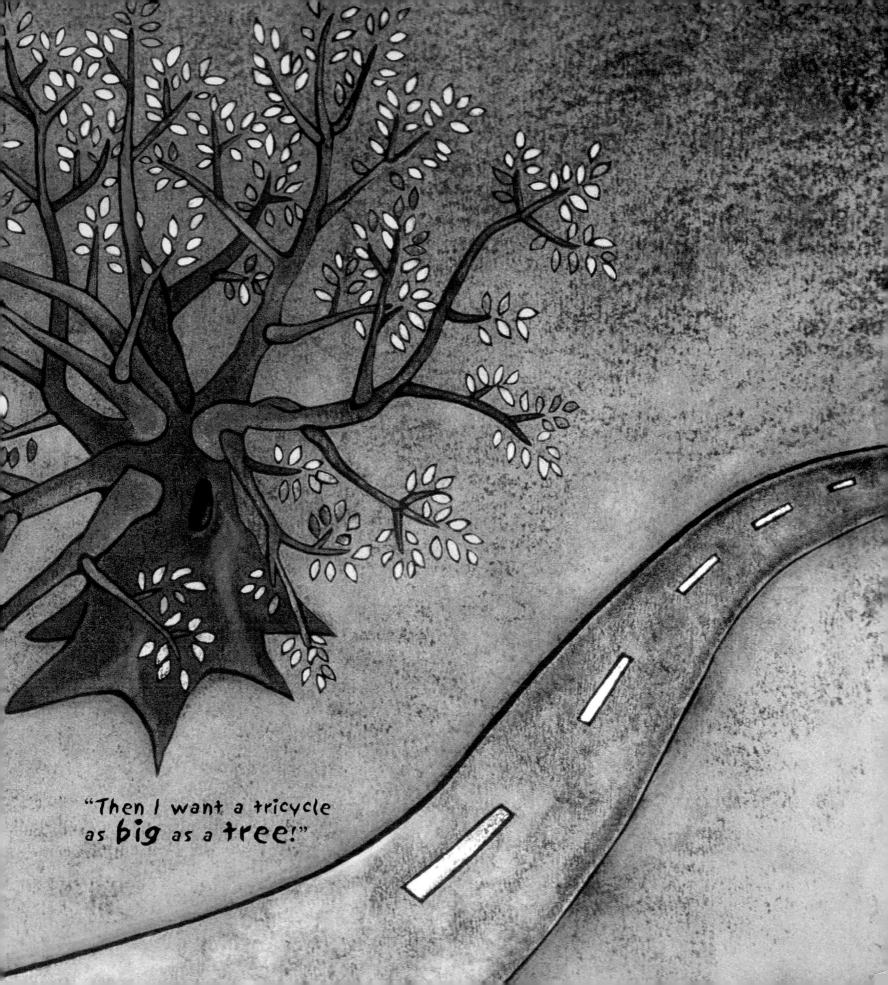

"Then I want a tricycle as **big** as a **tree!**"

"No Carl, you can`t have that. We don`t have streets **big** enough to ride it in," said the king.

Carl became angry, "Can`t I at least have an **elephant** as **big** as a **house**?"

And he stamped his little feet, "Or I don`t want anything at all."

The king shook his head and said nothing.

Little Carl was upset.

"I'll never be as **tall** as everybody else," he thought.

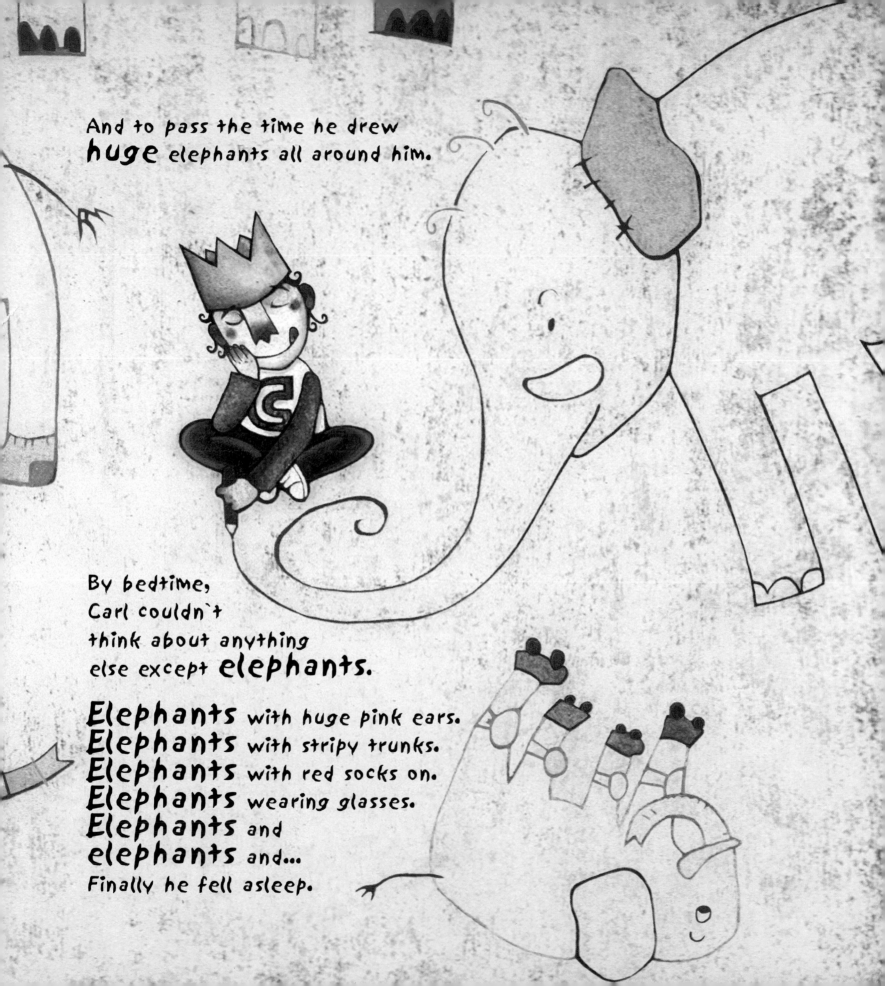

And to pass the time he drew **huge** elephants all around him.

By bedtime,
Carl couldn't
think about anything
else except **elephants.**

Elephants with huge pink ears.
Elephants with stripy trunks.
Elephants with red socks on.
Elephants wearing glasses.
Elephants and
elephants and...
Finally he fell asleep.

When Cort opened his eyes,
everything seemed strange.
Somehow it was all very **dark**.

He climbed out of bed to have a
look outside but all he could see
was a solid grey wall right in front
of the window.

So he walked downstairs and
opened the front door and he

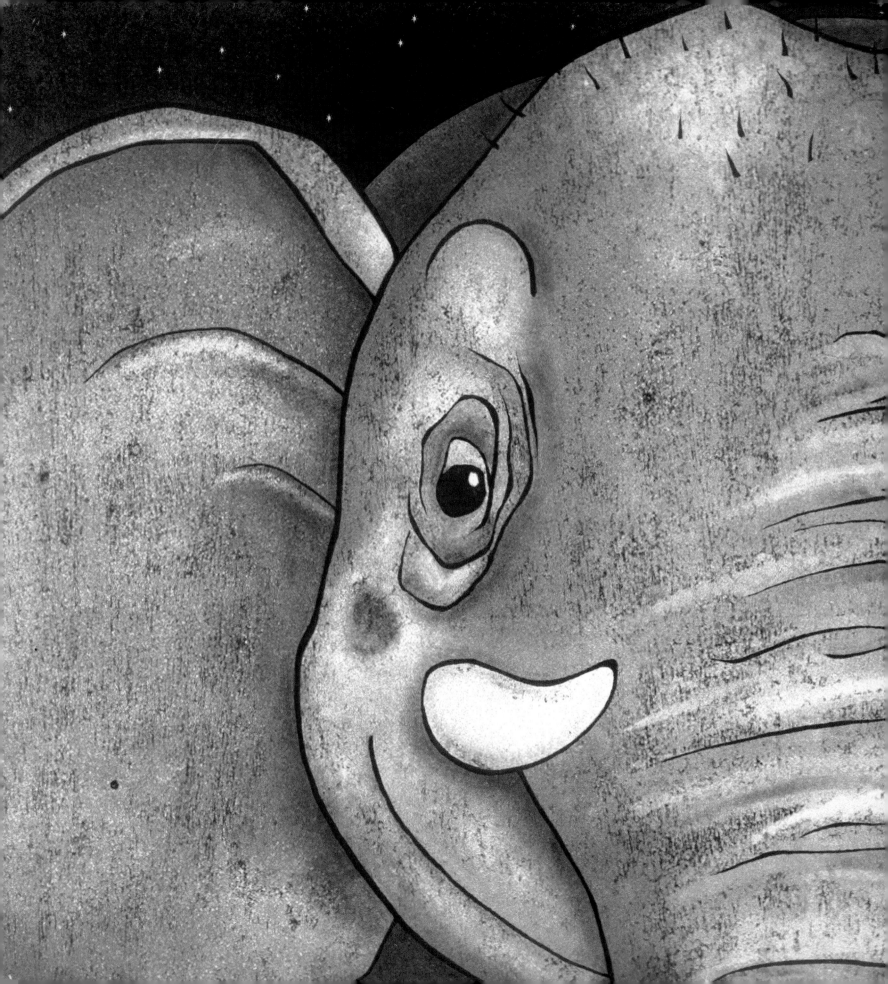

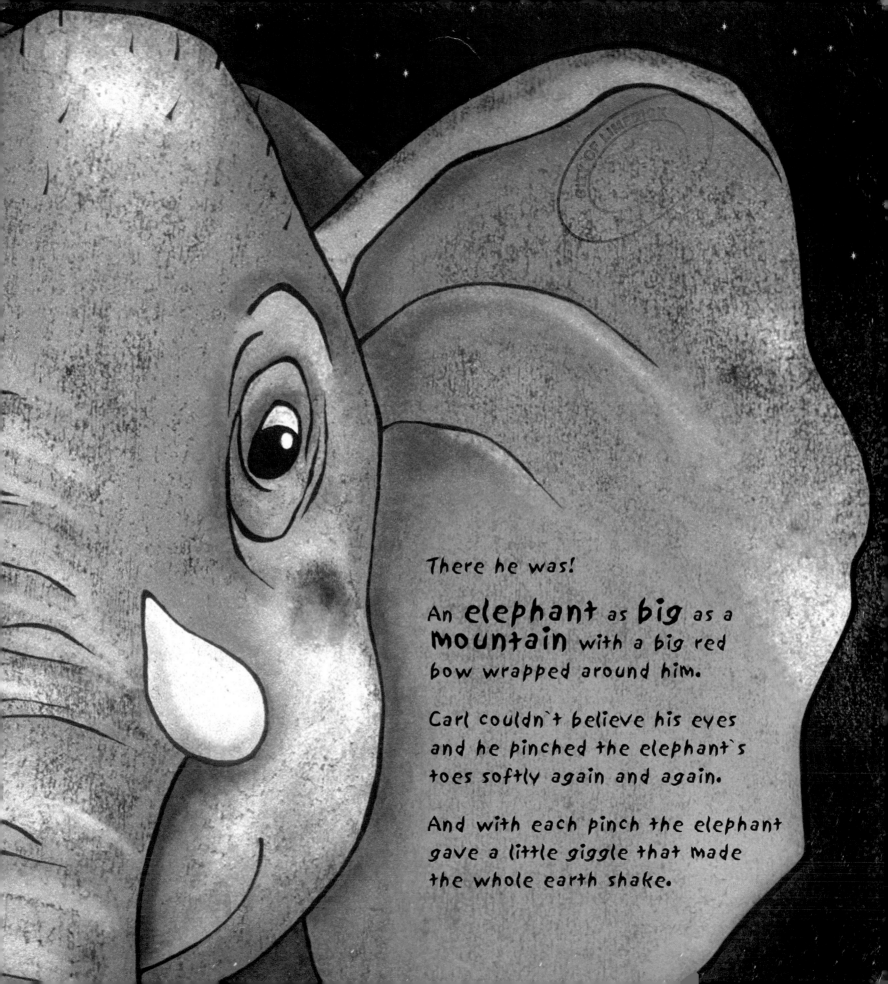

There he was!

An **elephant** as **big** as a **mountain** with a big red bow wrapped around him.

Carl couldn`t believe his eyes and he pinched the elephant`s toes softly again and again.

And with each pinch the elephant gave a little giggle that made the whole earth shake.

"I'm Archie," the *gigantic* elephant said.

"I'm Carl and it's my birthday today," said Carl. "Let's play hide and seek!"

Although it was still as dark as night, little Carl kept winning. Archie was so **big**, not even the castle could hide him. Carl and Archie played together for hours and hours.

"I'm so tired," whispered Carl finally.

"Oh," Archie said, "me too."

"Goodnight, little Carl," said Archie and
he waved farewell with his big red bow.

"Goodnight, Archie," said Carl sleepily.
"What a strange birthday!" he thought
to himself.

Little Carl crept into his bed.
He had never felt so tired.

Soon he fell asleep. He dreamt of all the wonderful things they would do together, next time Archie came to visit.

The next morning the king was waiting for Carl downstairs and there was a HUGE cake on the breakfast table.

"Happy birthday, little Carl," he said.

"But ..." little Carl stuttered, "my birthday was yesterday and you missed it. It was dark all day long and nobody was around – except for Archie."

Puzzled, the king looked at little Carl and said, "Who's Archie? You must have been dreaming.

It's your birthday today. Would you like your present now?"

"Look outside, little Carl!" the king said.

And there he was! A little elephant with a big red bow wrapped around him. He wasn`t as **big** as a MOUNTAIN - he was only about as tall as three large pieces of cheese piled on top of each other.

The little elephant gave little Carl a cheeky smile and said, "Hello – from Papa!"

Carl was very happy. He didn't want to be **tall** any more.

He was happy just as he was, because little Archie was really, really little, **just like him.**